JENNY AND THE
WRECKERS

JENNY AND THE WRECKERS

by
FAY SAMPSON
Illustrated by Vanessa Julian-Ottie

Marshall Pickering

Pickering and Inglis
Marshall Pickering
3 Beggarwood Lane, Basingstoke, Hants
RG23 7LP, UK

First published in Great Britain 1984
by Hamish Hamilton Children's Books
Copyright © 1984 by Fay Sampson
Illustrations copyright © 1984 by
Vanessa Julian-Ottie

First published in 1988 by Pickering and Inglis Ltd
Part of the Marshall Pickering Holdings Group
A subsidiary of the Zondervan Corporation

ISBN: 0 7208 0734 4

Text Set in Baskerville by
Katerprint Co. Ltd., Oxford
Printed and bound in Great Britain by
Anchor Brendon Ltd, Tiptree, Essex

This book is based on a true story

Dedicated to Annie Priestley

Chapter 1

THE SPRAY STRUCK the window like a handful of stones. Jenny started awake. Another gust rattled against the lighthouse cottage. But she was not frightened. The wind was lively, but it could do far worse than this. It could send huge waves shooting to the top of the cliff, a wall of water smacking into the lighthouse. The storm could tug at the roof as if it would lift the heavy slates off and hurl them half across Cornwall. This was nothing.

7

She snuggled deeper under the blanket. It was dark and warm in the little box bed against the wall. She could hear the waves crashing against the cliff and feel the slight shudder of the cottage with each shock. It did not worry Jenny. Those breakers had rocked her to sleep every winter since her mother died.

All the same, it must be nearly morning, or the rain would not have woken her. She poked her head out to see.

There was no glow from the smothered fire of the kitchen where she slept. It was dark outside the window. Then the gloom lightened as the great lantern swung round towards the sea. Light. Darkness. Darkness. Light. Dark. Dark. Light. Dark. Dark. Light. She counted the slowly passing seconds between the flashes. All night

the lantern had been turning on its
gleaming, oiled bearings. All night the
fierce Argand lamp had been burning
overhead, so bright in the lamp room

that she could not bear to look at it. But out at sea it was no more than a tiny spark of warning, glimpsed between mountainous waves and flying spray. Keep off, it said. Keep off my rocks. Here is danger.

The gloom became lighter between the flashes. It must be nearly morning. Soon her father would be coming down the winding staircase, stiff and sleepy. All night he had to stay awake to mind the lamp. He dare not close his eyes for more than a few minutes. He must not fall asleep. If the lamp went out there would be no light flashing and darkening above the rocks. The ships on their way to harbour would sail too close against the cliff. They would strike on the rocks and break and sink. And their crews would drown in the wild waves.

On Monday, Alan Squire would be

back from Bodmin with his new bride. But till then her father had no assistant keeper. The nights were long in January. He must be very lonely while Jenny slept.

She heard his footstep on the stairs. Quickly she jumped out of bed in her flannel nightdress. The floor was cold under her feet. She ran across to the fire and plunged the poker into its heart. The black coals broke apart. Inside was a glowing, living pulse that sprang into flame. She had the kettle over the fire and was getting the frying pan out as her father came into the kitchen.

"That's right, my pretty maid," he said with a grateful smile as he saw her breaking eggs and adding the last of the bacon to the pan. He always called her his pretty maid.

He rubbed his hands. "I'm ready for

that. There'll not be much cooking on shipboard today. The wind's building. It's from the north west. It'll be driving them down on to us if they don't stand off and turn for harbour."

Jenny served him his breakfast and sat down to her own. She had known already from the rattling rain on the window that the wind was north west. That was the danger wind. Most of the strong gales of Cornwall came from the south west. They buffeted the back of the cottage, where it was sheltered by the gorse-grown downs. But the windows faced north across the restless sea. And when the gales came that way, the cliffs stood right across the path of the racing ships.

It was grey dawn outside. Her father's head began to nod over his mug of tea.

13

"Time to turn in," he said. "My watch below."

She took the greasy plates away and shook the crumbs from the tablecloth. He would not go to bed just yet. There was something to be done first.

The lighthouse keeper walked across to a glass-fronted cupboard in the corner of the room. He inspected his hands to make sure they were clean. Then, carefully, he opened the door and lifted out a massive heavy object wrapped in green velvet cloth.

He laid this parcel on the table. It was so thick that now Jenny could hardly see over the top of it. But her father lifted her on to his knee and gently opened the velvet cloth. Even though it happened every morning, this was always the moment at which Jenny held her breath.

Inside was a book. It was the only book in the whole cottage. But what a book. The cover was of red leather, patterned in gold. When her father lifted the cover, the first thing you saw were the end papers in swirling patterns of green and blue, like oil on sunlit water. And then the stories began. The book was so enormous that it seemed to Jenny there must be enough stories in it to read one a day for the rest of her life. And in the heart of it was something very special. She reached out her hand.

"Did you wash your fingers?" asked her father.

"Of course I did!" He always asked, just to remind her how special this book was. As if she didn't know that for herself.

It was the great family Bible. His fingers found for her the place she wanted. Past the middle, where the Old Testament ended and the New Testament began. A double page that had no printing on it. Once, when the book was new, those pages must have stood white and empty. She imagined how it must have felt to pick up a pen and write in it for the first time:

Edward Trenear m. Ruth Annis 1786

Now it was a treasure-house of names. They were written in many different, bold hands. The ink of the first names was turning to brown, and the fine, white pages beginning to yellow at the edges. She traced her finger down the page without touching it and found near the bottom:

James m. Alice Penhaligon
b.1880   b.1884 died 1912

Her father and her mother.

And last of all, on a line by itself:

Jenifer
b.1907

Her own name. Her name, in this great book.

Her father turned the pages back to the stories. He read about David and Goliath. The story told how a young shepherd boy went to the battle front to take food to his brothers. But because he was so brave he found himself facing a great giant of a man in armour. They had a single combat, and the little shepherd boy with a sling and a stone beat the giant with his sword.

When the story was over and they had said their morning prayers, James Trenear undressed and went to bed. Jenny busied herself about the kitchen, sweeping, dusting, getting the dinner ready. And all the time the wind was getting stronger and the rain and the spray came lashing against the light-house harder and harder, as though they were trying to break in.

Chapter 2

JAMES TRENEAR LOOKED out of the window at the lashing rain. He pulled a face as he reached down his oilskin coat from the hook on the door.

"It's a wild, wet day for a three-mile walk. But there's no help for it. There's hardly a bite of food left in the cupboard. And it's Sunday tomorrow. I shall have to go shopping."

Jenny stood on tiptoe to reach her

own sou'wester. But her father stopped her.

"No, not you, my pretty maid. There's no sense in two of us getting soaked to the skin. I shall go quicker on my own this weather."

Disappointed, she watched him button his oilskins, tie on his sou'wester and gather up a leather bag. Those Saturday afternoon visits were special. They walked down into the village together to do the week's shopping, with sweets for Jenny and a smoke and a long chat for her father with the shopkeeper. It was a lonely life in a lighthouse. They had few friends. And Alan Squire had been a week away.

He saw her face and gave her a strong hug.

"Never fear. I'll be back as quick as I can. I'll be down in the village in two

shakes of duck's tail, with this wind blowing behind me. But it'll be a hard fight back, if it goes on rising like this."

He lifted the latch. The storm crashed the door back against the wall before he could catch it, letting in a great blast of wind and wet. He turned quickly.

"Don't you worry, though, pretty maid. I'll be home before dark to light the lantern, whatever happens. There'll be lives depending on it tonight." And he heaved the door shut behind him.

Jenny ran to the window. She saw him stagger round the corner of the cottage. Then the wind whipped him from her sight.

There was a sudden loneliness in the lighthouse kitchen. Worse than she remembered for a long time. It seemed oddly silent, in spite of the waves break-

ing with an unending roar against the cliffs and the gale thundering over the slates. It was not the peaceful, friendly silence that she felt in bed, with her father upstairs in the lamproom. Or the busy daytime quiet when she tiptoed round the kitchen trying not to wake him as he slept.

She went across to the corner cupboard and stood looking at the great family Bible, wrapped in its velvet cloth. She would have liked to open the door and lift it down. To touch its rich covers for comfort. To open the pages and read her mother's name again. But she did not dare. It was the one precious thing they had. Only her father unwrapped it, morning and evening, and read it to her. And even then, she hardly dared to touch it.

She moved back to the window. She

could only just see the edge of the cliff through the driving rain. She wished her father would come back.

Chapter 3

JAMES TRENEAR HAD his head down, battling up the slope of the downs. He had to struggle against the gale as well, with a heavy bag of groceries on his back. The wind was like a rushing broom. It was trying to sweep him back into the rain-washed streets of the village he had just left. The rain had almost stopped now, but the lighthouse keeper was as wet inside his oilskins as out. The air was pricking with salt as huge gusts of spray were

28

flung inland over the edge of the cliff.

James Trenear was worried. It was
getting dark too soon. The sky was a
mass of flying clouds. And the wind was
rising to storm force, so that he could
hardly walk against it. He tried to

hurry. Jenny was alone in the light-house cottage. And with the night closing in so fast the lamp should soon be lit. There would be ships in danger tonight even with the light flashing out its warning. But if the lantern was dark, the cliffs waited like the sharp teeth of a tiger. They would tear in pieces any boat that sailed too close.

A stone rattled down the path towards him. The rain must be starting to wash away the path. He forced his way on a few more steps. More stones came tumbling towards him. He stop-ped and peered up. There was no one there. Only the clumps of gorse bushes beside the path. On he went. Those bushes would shelter him only a little longer. Once he was past them the wind would really catch him.

Suddenly he was whirled round. But

it was not the wind. There were yells in his ears. Then the darkness he had been dreading came all at once.

He was lying face down on the wet path. There was a great weight on his back. Sharp ropes twisted round his arms, forcing them behind him. His ankles were tied. He struggled to look up and a gag went round his mouth.

He could see boots. Muddy breeches. The dripping skirts of greatcoats. He heard a hollow panting. He turned his head sideways and squinted upwards in the gloom.

There were bogey figures all around him. They were muffled in coats and scarves. And on their heads they had wicker things, like pointed beehives. their voices came thickly from inside these baskets.

"Is he out cold?"

"Not he. Look, he's watching us."

"Does he know us, do you think?"

"Should have hit him harder. He wouldn't tell no tales then."

"What do you say? Do we give him a push over the cliff? Could have stumbled easy in this storm. Take the ropes off, nobody would know."

"Waves might wash him right up to Bude. Nothing to do with us."

The lighthouse keeper was helpless. He shut his eyes and groaned.

"He won't trouble us. What can he tell, anyway? He hasn't seen a face. So long as the lantern is dead tonight, that's all we want."

"Aye. Get that bonfire going along the cliff. Lead them a mile off course. There'll be good pickings by morning."

"Lucky we covered the wood up. This wind'll whip up a fair old blaze."

"Quick. Shove him under the gorse bushes."

The thorns scratched his face as they pushed him under the branches. Then their boots tramped past him, on, away up the path. He was alone in the howling storm, unable to move. The last of the light was fading from the sky.

Chapter 4

JENNY WENT TO the window for the twentieth time. The clock on the mantelpiece said four o'clock. But it was almost pitch-dark inside the room. At last she lit the oil lamp and carried it across to the window-sill. She knew it was silly. Fishermen's wives burned lights in their windows to guide the boats home at night. But her father was not coming from the sea.

The rain no longer beat against the panes. But the cottage shook with the

36

pounding waves below, and there was a sharp crackle of spray.

She sat by the fire. Her father did not come. Presently she got up and laid the table. She was more worried now. It was fully dark outside. Her little lamp still burned on the window-sill. But up

in the lantern room of the lighthouse, the great light still waited to be lit. It waited for the flame to hiss and roar. For the mirrors to catch its sparkle in a thousand frames. For the huge wheel to start turning on its polished bearings, sending the light circling round the windows. Flash. Dark. Dark. Flash. Signalling to the ships to keep away.

But the wheels were still. And the lamp was dark. The lighthouse was dead.

Jenny knew how important that lantern was. All her life the lighting of the lamp had come before anything else. Whatever they were doing, wherever they went, the keeper on duty must always be back to light the lantern. By day he kept the great machinery oiled and polished, the windows and mirrors clean, the cans full of oil. By night he kept the lamp burning and turning.

It was growing late. And the storm was raging outside. Her father must come home to light the lamp. He must.

There was a worse enemy than darkness for the ships at sea. On the shore there were wreckers. If the lighthouse failed, they could make a false fire on the cliffs. The ships would set their course by it. But instead of finding safety, they would crash into the rocks. The timbers would split apart. Their cargo would be washed up on the beach. When day broke, the wreckers would seize and steal it. And all the people on the ships would be drowned.

Her father must come home. Soon. Before it was too late.

But Jenny's father lay in the mud struggling and groaning. He could not work his hands free. The cold struck

through his wet clothes, chilling him to the bone. Only the thick gorse bushes kept the wind from freezing him.

He rolled desperately over on to his back and looked up through the branches that crossed his face. The night was utterly black. There was not one star to be seen. The air was full of rushing clouds, darker than the sky they hid. He twisted round to where the lighthouse should be. He gazed into the darkness, hoping against hope to see its bright beam stabbing out across the sea.

But there was no beam, no signal of warning. It was as though the lighthouse was not there.

If only Alan was not away in Bodmin. If only his wife Alice was still alive. She would have lit the lantern. If only Jenny was older and taller.

But his little maid was alone in the lighthouse. And she would never be able to light the lantern by herself. He clenched his fists and prayed for help.

Chapter 5

AT FIVE O'CLOCK Jenny picked up the
oil-lamp from the window-sill. As she
opened the door that led into the foot of
the lighthouse, she felt guilty. She was
never allowed here alone. It was not a
place to play in. Always there had been
someone beside her, or up there in the
lantern room. Her father or Alan.
Someone else who was in charge. Someone else who polished and oiled the
machinery and kept it turning. Someone else who lit the great hissing, flaring

lantern and sent its light out across the
sea.

Now the whole lighthouse was dead
and dark. The wind shook the walls.
The sea howled against the cliffs. And
out in that storm, ships battled against
the waves. In the bows there would be
look-outs trusting to the lighthouse to
give them warning of danger. But no
one had lit the lantern.

Jenny's small lamp threw shadows
shooting across the white-washed room.
Here stood the great casks of oil from
which the lantern was filled. She
climbed the first stone stair. In the next
room there was a plain table and a
chair. Here her father sat and wrote his
log-book. He noted down the ships that
passed the lighthouse. The great clip-
pers all the way from Australia, bound
for Bristol. The sturdy steamers chug-

ging out into the Atlantic and away to the far coast of America.

On summer mornings she had stood beside that table gazing out at the bright sea and the racing ships, and wished herself on board. She had felt herself turning her face to meet the breeze and the spray. She had longed to climb the rigging and balance a hundred feet above the waves like a bird in the tree-tops. She had imagined herself in the crow's nest, shading her eyes and shouting 'Land-ho!'

But not tonight. She did not want to imagine herself on board now. She did not want to climb the mast in a raging gale and reef the thundering sail. She did not want to cling to the wet deck as the waves crashed over the rail. She did not want the sick fear in her stomach as she waited for the rocks to tear out the keel.

She went on up. The steps were wooden now. They brought her into the lantern room. It was ghostly tonight, this room which should never be dark. The light from her lamp flashed on polished brass and sparkled in reflecting prisms of glass. But outside, the storm threw darkness against the clear windows as though it was trying to break in.

She set down the lamp on the floor. The great Argand lantern rose in the middle of the room. There was the huge disc that kept it turning, smoothly, effortlessly swinging the light past the shutters that made it flash and darken, darken and flash, hour after hour as it rolled round. She touched it with her finger, knowing the feeling of power it would give her. One small push and the whole lantern began to swing round. It

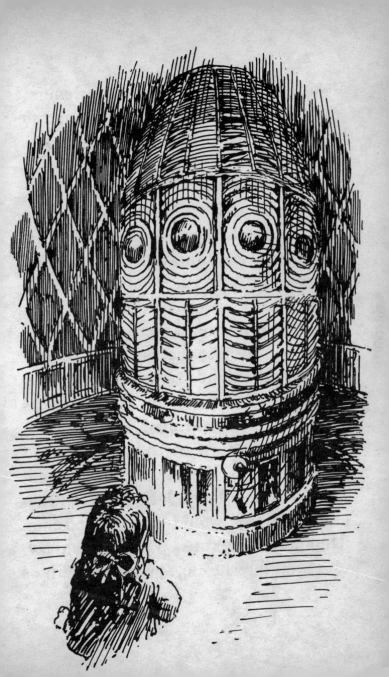

always thrilled her that she, Jenifer, could set this vast machinery moving so lightly. It was for this that the keepers watched over it so lovingly, oiling it, testing it, so that it should never fail.

But high above that was the lantern itself. It lived within a palace of glass. The glass was beautifully ribbed and layered and curved. There were hundreds of rows of prisms in eight great panes, closing the lantern round. And every one of those pieces of glass would catch up the light and send it sparkling up or down or sideways, so that all its power was concentrated into one brilliant beam that swung round and round, over the downs and the cliffs and the sea. Flash, Dark. Dark. Flash. From miles away it would give its warning. Here are dangerous rocks. Keep away.

Trembling a little, she stood on tiptoe

and opened the glass panels. She looked at the lamp itself. It was not so very different from the one she had carried up from the kitchen. The brass pipes that carried the oil. The glass chimney. But it was immensely bigger. She could not even reach the chimney or the jet where her father lit the flame.

As she sank back on to her heels she felt a sense of relief. She was not sure why she had felt driven to come all the way up here in the darkness. Her father was very late, but he must be home soon. He would light the lantern. She ought not to be here alone. She should not have touched the glass. A lighthouse is not a toy for children. She should leave it to someone else who knew better.

But as she turned away, she felt the gale rage about the tower. And out at sea, there would be ships, caught in the storm, flying up the channel in the darkness.

Chapter 6

JENNY'S FATHER, LYING in the mud under the gorse-bushes, could not move. But further along the cliff people were busy.

"Get that fire blazing."

"Lucky the wood's stayed dry."

"Ben, you take one side of that tarpaulin. Harry, you catch hold of the other. Now, my handsomes. Walk in front of the fire. Stop there. Now, on you go. And back again."

"There! Proper old lighthouse us

have made! Flash. Dark. Dark. Flash. You'd never tell it from the real one."

"And now us waits. Like a conger-eel in the rocks. Waiting for what will swim into our jaws. There'll be wrecks tonight."

"And good pickings on the beach before morning."

The lighthouse kitchen seemed even more lonely now. The clock ticked on the mantelpiece. The coals rustled as the fire in the grate burned lower. The scuttle was nearly empty. It was pitch-dark outside, and the house creaked in the gale that was raging around the walls.

At last Jenny could stand it no longer. She ran out of the house, feeling the door snatched from her hand as she opened it.

In a moment of terror, she thought

she had dashed off the cliff. The sea was coming right over the path to meet her. Although the rain had stopped, she was drenched with spray and the wind whipped her breath away so that she was almost suffocated. She turned to the west, fighting to keep her feet on the slippery ground. And she saw what she had feared to see.

Flash. Dark. Dark. Flash. There was a light along the cliff. The lighthouse above her head was dead and dark. For the first time in her life the great revolving lantern was still. The piercing beam was not sending out its warning across the sea. And another light had taken its place.

It was sending out a false message. "Here is the headland. Beyond me there is safe harbour." And it wasn't true. Beyond that light was the real

headland, the jagged rocks, the hungry breakers.

Jenny ran indoors sobbing and slammed the door. She sat down at the table and found that she was shivering all over. She was wet and cold and frightened. She wanted more than anything else in the world for her father to come home and take her in his arms and then go upstairs and light the lantern. But he did not come.

Gradually she stopped crying. The clock still ticked softly. She needed something to comfort her. She carried a chair across to the corner of the room and opened the cupboard. She had to stand on a chair to lift the Bible down. It was so huge and thick that it needed both her arms to hold it. She had to be very careful as she stepped down from the chair.

Clutching the heavy parcel to her, she carried it to the table and unwrapped the velvet cloth. The great family Bible lay in front of her. It was the first time she had opened it by herself. She sat down on the chair and looked at the leather cover for a while. Then she plucked up the courage to take a handful of pages and turn them over.

The book seemed to fall open by itself. As if the words on that page wanted to come out and speak to her. She traced them with her finger, forgetting that in her hurry and fright she had not washed her hands. The words stood out strong and clear from the white page.

"God is our refuge and strength,
a very present help in trouble."

She read them out in a shaking voice. And then again more strongly. She went on.

"Therefore we will not fear, though
the earth be removed, and though the
mountains be carried into the midst
of the sea;

Though the waters thereof roar and be troubled."

And as she read, she began to feel braver and warmer. The firelit room seemed not so lonely as before. After a while she turned to the place between the Old and New Testament where the family tree was written.

James m. Alice

and then their child

Jenifer

All the Trenears. Lighthouse keepers, fishermen and women. All her family who had worked on the coast of Cornwall, looking to the sea for a living and to the shore for safety. And she was the last of their line. For a long time she stared at their names. And then she knew what she must do.

Chapter 7

IT WAS MORE frightening going up the
lighthouse stairs the second time, knowing what was in front of her. Behind, in
the warm kitchen, the red Bible was
still lying open on the table – old and
comforting. But the lantern room was
cold and dark and lonely, and if she
made a mistake she might do some
terrible damage. At a bend in the stair
she nearly turned back. And then she
saw through a window the gleam of fire
along the cliffs. Flash. Dark. Flash.

With a cry she ran up the last few steps. Suppose a ship had seen that signal. Suppose it had turned and was steering now towards the headland. Suppose it was already too late.

The glass lantern was a sleeping giant, full of enormous power. She set down her own small lamp in a corner of the room. At once the shadows on the walls stopped trembling and settled into steady patterns. The brass of the oil pipes gleamed softly. The glass panels glinted. But nothing else would happen unless she did it herself.

And then she remembered she had not brought any matches.

Almost crying at her own silliness, she ran to the door, only to be stopped short by the darkness on the stairs. Of course! She had forgotten to pick up her little oil lamp. And as she went back to

the corner where she had set it down, laughter and relief suddenly warmed her. She would not need matches, after all. She had brought her own flame with her. Only a small one, beside the towering Argand lantern. But a small flame can grow into a huge one. All she needed was one of the long, slender wax tapers her father used. She found a bundle of them, wrapped in oiled paper. They were well looked after and ready to use, like everything else her father kept in the lantern room. The taper was like a thin candle. It would make her arm reach just a little bit further. Would it be far enough?

She stood on tiptoe and pushed the glass shutter back, feeling again the easy, oiled movement. For a moment, she felt strong and powerful.

Inside there were more brass pipes,

leading to the wick where the flame must burn. Below was the oil-tank. She knew she did not have to worry about that. Her father always kept it full and ready. She only had to light the lamp.

There was a brass wheel near the end of the oil pipe. She knew she must turn this and let the oil soak up into the wick. It was like the one on the kitchen lamp, only much bigger. She could not be wrong.

But this was the moment she was frightened of. When she touched the machinery she had always been forbidden to play with. Then a quick glance over her shoulder showed the false light leaping out from the cliff, luring sailors to their death. She had to do it. She was her father's daughter. There was no one else to do his work. Straining with all

her might, she reached her arm deep into the glass dome.

It was no use. She was not tall enough. Even though she stood as high on her toes as she could, and stretched her arm till the muscles seemed to be tearing from their socket, she could not reach that wheel. And without it, the oil would not rise and the wick would not burn.

She wondered if she could haul herself right inside the lantern. But she was afraid to lean on the glass panels, afraid to put her weight on the slender pipes. What if she damaged the lantern?

But she was determined now. She would not be beaten. All she needed was something to make her tall enough to reach. She looked round hurriedly. But there was nothing to stand on. The lantern room was kept tidy and bare of everything except what was absolutely needed. There was not a box, not a chair. Nothing that she could use. She would have to go down to the room below.

This time she remembered to take the lamp. Her heart was beating fast now, but she knew what she must do. She must fetch the wooden chair that her father sat on to write his log-book. She must do everything as quickly and sensibly as possible, and try not to think about the ships racing towards the rocks in the darkness.

It was only when she stood in the lower room and picked up the chair that she realised she could not carry the lamp as well. She could feel the panic beginning to rise in her again. Nothing was going right. But she fought against it and made herself take the lamp back

to the top of the stairs where the light would reach as far as the first turn to guide her. When she went back for the chair she had to fumble for it in the darkness. But the stabbing light along the cliff kept her courage strong. She would not let the wreckers beat her.

It was not a big chair, but it was heavy for Jenny to carry. She struggled with it to the steps, and put it down, panting. The next part was much harder. Feeling with her foot for the next stair in the darkness, with only a gleam of light on the wall above her head. Then hauling herself and the chair up higher. The stairs began to turn and the legs jammed against the wall.

She fought them free, almost falling backwards down the steps, and staggered on. But halfway up she could go no further. She had to stop and rest.

Not for long. She found that resting was worse than working. Nightmare pictures raced through her mind. If only she knew what was happening out at sea. What if the moments she was wasting meant the difference between life and death? She picked up the chair that she had wedged between her knees and the wall.

Once she could see the light it was suddenly easier. The chair seemed lighter. She was at the top of the stairs. Now all she had to do was to set it in front of the lantern and climb on the seat.

It was dangerous, leaning in over the pipes. Difficult to know where to rest her weight. But she could reach at last. She turned the wheel, praying that she was doing the right thing. It was a little stiffer than the glass shutters, but it moved for her. She set it fully open, and then turned it back a little, afraid to release too much power.

With her heart thudding in her chest, she stepped back on to the floor. Now she was ready to light the flame.

Chapter 8

THIS WAS THE moment she had been pushing to the back of her mind. She had been covering up her dread of it by keeping busy. Hurrying up and down stairs. Moving the lamp, carrying the chair. Now it had come. She could not put it off any longer.

She must light the taper from the small lamp. She must climb on to the chair. She must reach into the lantern and set the flame against the wick.

This was what she was afraid of. She

did not know what would happen then. She had watched her father do it many times. Her heart had leaped in excitement as the flame roared in the glass chimney and then settled to a steady pulse, and the shutters were closed and the lantern set turning around, and the signal went out across the sea. But she had never had to do it herself. Watching was not the same as doing. What if she had left something out, or turned something too far? What would happen then when she lit the flame? Would the fire go roaring out of control, burning the lighthouse, shattering the glass, exploding the oil? Should she even think of lighting it by herself, with nobody there to help her?

"Oh, God, help me!" she prayed.

For a moment she stood listening, longing to hear at last her father's

footstep on the stairs. But all she heard was the murderous gale, making the walls creak and the windows shudder. There was only Jenny to save the ships.

Her hand was not quite steady as she lifted the glass chimney from the kitchen lamp and held the taper above the small blue flame. It wobbled about so that it seemed to take an age to catch. But at last a bold yellow light sprang up from the end of the taper, smoking slightly. She let it steady, and then carried it carefully to the chair. If she moved too fast the draught might blow it out. She would have liked to set it down somewhere while she climbed up on to the chair. But she was afraid that the taper might overbalance and set fire to something. So she held it very carefully away from her clothes while she got up, first on to her knees and then standing. She reached deep into the lantern and up.

Such a tiny, yellow flame, with a blue heart. Just one spark, reflected a thousand times in the glass lenses. And within that flame was the power to light the whole lantern with its brilliant beam. The light from that one taper in her hand would go singing out across miles of sea. This was her moment of glory.

She stretched on tiptoe as far as she could reach. Just a little bit further . . .

And then she overbalanced. For an awful moment she felt herself falling into the lantern. She dropped to her knees on the chair, clutching at the rim of the glass. The whole construction shook and she shut her ears, waiting for it to come crashing down in pieces.

But the world steadied, and she clambered off the chair, bruised and shaken. The taper had fallen deep into the machinery. Mercifully, it had gone out. Behind her, the little oil lamp flared and smoked without its chimney. She set it straight. She was shaking all over, worse than before.

She did not dare to climb on the chair again. She must find something bigger to stand on. She wanted more than anything to run back to the kitchen, to

jump into her little bed and huddle there, waiting for her father to return. But she must finish what she had started now.

There was a table downstairs. She did not know how she could possibly carry it up the steps. But she would have to try.

She ran down to the room below for the second time. She bumped into the table and put her arms round it. It was hard to know how to get hold of it. She staggered a few steps. The weight of it dragged her down. It was no good. She could not even get it to the foot of the staircase. She could not possibly lift it higher.

Quick! Think of something else. If she had something to stand on. Something thick and solid to put on the seat of the chair. She only needed to be a little bit taller. Gasping for breath now, she ran back to the top of the stairs and picked up the lantern. Down again, searching the room, but there was nothing else there. On down, the lamp flashing round the curved walls. Across the storeroom, with its casks of oil. Into the cottage.

The kitchen was welcoming. The fire purred in the grate. The Bible lay open on the table. She wanted to stay here. But that was not why she had come. was not why she had come.

There were more chairs. What if she stood one on top of another? She lifted her own on to her father's. But she saw at once that it would not do.

She looked frantically round. There must be something she could use. Something small enough for her to carry up the stairs. Something strong enough to bear her weight. Something she could put on top of the chair. If only they had a little stool. Even a log of wood. She searched in every corner and every cupboard. But there was nothing that would do.

At last she sank down on to the chair in front of the table, lowered her head on to her arms and began to cry.

Chapter 9

A SHARP CORNER was digging into Jenny's elbow. She tried to push it aside without looking, but it was too heavy to move. She rubbed the tears from her eyes and looked up.

The great, family Bible lay on the table beside her. Its red leather cover was warm and friendly. She put out her hand and touched it for comfort. It was big and strong like her father. And yet she could put her arms round it and carry it.

A thought shot through her mind.

Oh, no! She would not dare. The Bible was the most precious thing they had. She was barely allowed to touch it with clean hands. Surely she must not dream of standing on it? Suppose she dirtied it? Suppose she dropped it? Suppose the pages broke away from the cover? Surely her father would be angry with her?

But the book was there beside her. It

seemed to be speaking to her. As she fingered the pages, she remembered the story her father had read that morning. How little David had beaten the giant Goliath with the help of a sling and a stone.

"God is my refuge and strength,
a very present help in trouble."

She whispered the words to herself. She needed all the help in the world if she was to beat the wreckers. And she must beat them. She must send the light beaming out through the storm. She must do her father's work.

Before she had time to lose her courage, she picked up the book and almost ran to the door. The thick Bible was nearly as heavy as the chair, but it was so much easier to carry. She could hold it, with her arms tight round it, hugging it to her chest. It did not drag against the walls. She felt its solid warmth pressing against her, as though it wanted to give her strength.

She almost forgot the lamp, but she managed to clutch it in front of her. The light led her up the stairs. Her arms were aching but she did not stop. She had lost too much time already. She put the book on the chair. Now she would be tall enough. She knew that she could trust it to bear her weight. It was strong enough for anything. Edward, Ruth, James, Alice. They had all trusted it. Their names were in the book. Now all the Trenears were under her feet, holding her up, adding their strength to the strength that was in that book. And she was a Trenear. She was one of them.

She reached out the second taper with a steady hand. There was a little jet that would carry the flame inside the

chimney. And suddenly she was seeing clearly what it was her father did every night when he lit the lantern. It was as though he was guiding her hand. She knew she was doing it right, and she could feel the strength flowing into her from under her feet.

The flames hissed, small and blue. Then with a roar it sprang into the lantern chimney. For a moment Jenny knew fear, but only for a moment. The flame steadied and she turned the brass wheel till it stood straight and lovely.

And all around her was a miracle. Thousands of flames, brilliant and beautiful, mirrored at her out of all the glass prisms. Thousands of lights, clear, bright, singing, winging out of the windows, so that the darkness was flooded with radiance far stronger than any signal the wreckers could send.

She climbed down from the chair and moved the lever that would set the machinery going. The great turntable began to revolve. Flash. Dark. Dark. Flash. Dark. Dark. Flash. Dark. Dark. Flash. On and on into the howling night. The headland was safe. The warning light was flashing. The ships would sail past and come home to harbour.

Chapter 10

JAMES TRENEAR LIFTED his head from the mud again and groaned. He called for help. But there was no one to hear. Then he blinked. Was the night playing tricks with his eyes? Flash. Dark. Dark. Flash. The sky was shot with brilliance that came and went and came again. Surely that could not be the wreckers' fire, so bright, so steady?

There were running feet on the path above. People rushing back down to the village. He heard shouts and cursing coming towards him.

"Who lit it, then?"

"Keeper couldn't have got free."

"There's nobody there but his little maid."

"We'll be empty-handed tonight, curse it."

The voices went on down the path.

A shadow bent over the lighthouse keeper. A knife slit the rope. A husky voice, muffled under the mask, said, "Get home to your maid, then. And keep your mouth shut. We thought we'd got the best of you. But it seems there must be somebody helping your maid."

James Trenear limped towards the lighthouse on stiff and bruised legs. He was trying to understand how Jenny could have managed all by herself. It wasn't possible.

The kitchen was empty. He went up

the turning lighthouse stair to the very
top. In the middle of the lantern room,
Jenny lay curled up on the floor, asleep,
with her head resting on the Bible.

And over them both the light went
circling. Shining on and on until the
sunrise.

Other Marshall Pickering Paperbacks

The Long Summer   *Eleanor Watkins*

A sizzling hot summer holiday adventure for James, Katie and Paul. There has not been as much as a cloud in the sky for weeks, just sun and more sun. The stream has dried up and the earth is cracked and hard. On a farm camping holiday, a surprise discovery saves the animals and wildlife which are dying of thirst, but trapped by a raging hill fire themselves, the children remember the farmer telling them about the *Living Water*.

£1.60

The Ponies of Swallowdale Farm   *Sue Garnett*

Cassie loves horses more than anything else. Helping at Mrs. Cole's stables in return for free rides, she is heartbroken at her family's news that they are to move to the Lake District.

As they near their new rectory home, the beautiful mountain scenery turns Cassie's despair into delight. But it is short lived and all her hopes of ever riding again are dashed when she meets the stuck-up girl whose father owns the trekking stables nearby.

Why does she hate Cassie so much? Why, with all those horses, is she so miserable? Cassie *must* win her friendship, but how?

£1.75

All Alone (Except for my dog Friday) *Claire Blatchford*

'Dear Girl, go home'. Margaret found the note on her desk. Who had written it? Was it one of her friends she had had before she lost her hearing? They all seemed to ignore her now. In fact, Margaret was sure no-one understood what it was like to be deaf. Not her parents, nor even her brother, Frank. No one – except a lovable stray sheep-dog called Friday.

But the comfort he brings to Margaret is spoiled by her constant fears that his owners will come and claim him, and leave her – once again – all alone.

£1.60

The Music Plays Past Midnight *Marilyn Cram Donahue*

Syl both looked and felt a nobody. Wherever she went, if people weren't being rude or making fun at her, they just put up with her and hoped she'd go away. Caro felt sorry for her in a way, but drew the line at becoming friends. She could never live *that* down among the rest of the crowd. Yet Syl seemed so unhappy, she couldn't turn her back on her, and together, despite all the odds, they discover the best of friendships.

£1.60

The Fire Brand   *Jennifer Rees*

Jake, who had lived all his life in and out of a children's home, was on his way to yet another foster home. He had hated them all so far and was all ready to behave in his usual wild, rebellious way which had earned him his nickname – The Fire Brand.

But the Jarvis family turn out to be different from all the others, and Jake is surprised to find himself changing too.

In *The Fire Brand*, discover the reason for Jake's happy surprise.

95p

The Great Darkness   *Wendy Green*

What happens when a teenage boy from a primitive culture meets a girl from the computer age, after the world has been taken over by a robot government?

Together, Um and the girl defy the authority of 'the Box' and discover a new meaning to their lives.

£1.25